The Priest

The Picnic

The Priest

Secrets of a Dancing Girl
Book 5

by
Cecily Riley

The Priest

Secrets of a Dancing Girl
Book 5

ISSN 2515-1568

Text©2019 Cecily Riley
Illustrations©2019 Emily Woodthorpe

ISBN 978-1-908577-91-7

5 3 1 2 4
First Edition

British Library Cataloguing-in-Publication Data.
A catalogue record for this book is available
from the British Library.

Although loosely based on related events, any
reference to persons, living or dead, is purely
coincidental.

Hawkwood Books 2019

To every naughty girl in this world

❝What do you mean: you want to keep it?" I heard Ron, the stagehand, whisper excitedly in the darkened wings. "We're not even married! And I don't want to get married."

"But Ron," Tina pleaded. "We have to! I cannot get rid of it! It's against my religion."

"I don't care if it's against the weather, the tide or your religion! We had a good time and that's it!"

"But Ron, we were together, we are two people in this. Are you going to let me deal with this alone?" Tina said on the verge of tears.

"It's like I told you, my girl. We had a good time and now it's over. If you haven't been careful, it's not my problem."

"Careful? How?" Tina asked, openly if quietly sobbing.

"You girls know people, you can take care of it, if you want to. And, anyway, who says it's mine?"

"What? But I haven't been with anyone else."

"So you say! You dancing girls, you really are the racy type!" he said smugly. "The fifteen minutes bell has rung: I have to go... let me know if there are any doctor's bills."

1

Upon hearing those words, I felt my stomach knotting and my cheeks flushing. I knew from personal experience the utter despair that situation put a girl in. What a heel!

Ron walked out of the darkness and adjusted his belt as if something more than a conversation had taken place back there. That was the moment I chose to reveal myself. I stepped into the brackish blue light from the door recess where I had been eavesdropping. I stared him down as I played with the fringed end of my dressing gown's belt.

"Hello Luce," Ron said, barely concealing his surprise.

"How are you Ron?" I said, letting him know I had heard every word of their conversation and how I felt about his attitude towards Tina's predicament.

"All right, thanks," he muttered. "I got to dash, the fifteen minutes have rung."

"I heard. You should run. And make sure you don't trip on the way there," I said with every variation of threat in my voice.

He vanished swiftly towards the stage and the growing noise of the expectant crowd. Tina stepped out from behind the flat on cue. Her broad features were greyed with despair.

That was the moment I chose to reveal myself.

Her cheeks were bathed with tears and her black locks hung limply on the sides of her sorry face. She was already wearing her school uniform, but a tremendously racier version than English schoolgirls wore. It made an uncomfortable contrast with her despondent expression and demeanour.

As soon as she saw me and my sympathetic look, she threw herself into my arms and started wailing in earnest. I shushed her as best I could without being unfeeling and guided her towards the stairs of the dressing room. She fell heavily into the chair at her make-up table.

Flora, Norma, Greta and Bridget were already upstairs. And Tina really should've been upstairs also. Ethel and Jane were arguing, as usual, about a news article, which made a change. Mary, also as usual, pricked up as she identified the urgency of the situation and silently came to stand beside me. Over the last few weeks, her attitude towards me had gone back to what it used to be. I assumed it had to do with her relationship with her constable moving to a more physical plane.

Rose, the girl hired to replace Helen, was struggling with her costume but was too shy or too proud to ask for help. Our blonde aristocrat had vanished with a member of the Admiralty. We already had bets on when Mrs Huff would cut the newcomer down a size or make her cry.

But right now, it was one of our darling Germans who was crying. Her wails were heart wrenching and I felt quite at a loss as to how I could possibly help, other then making soothing sounds.

"What I am going to do?" Tina said in an English more tinged with her Teutonic roots then ever. "I am a fallen woman."

"Nonsense," I reasoned. "It happens to all of us, like a rite of passage. It'll be all right."

"How?" she practically barked at me.

"I don't know... if you can't have an abortion, then you'll have to work as long as you can..."

"And then?" she stared at me, her face unnaturally red.

"I don't know, to be honest. I am more the 'getting rid of it' kind of girl, you know."

"She could come to the St George Church shelter. They take care of women... in her condition," Mary whispered as if Tina was a very ill patient and not supposed to hear.

"Really?" Tina said, her eyes lighting up

with hope.

"Don't get your hopes up! It isn't the Ritz," Ethel said, having caught up with our conversation and stepped closer.

"As long as you don't go to Father Higgins, you're fine," said Rose, who, apparently, had been listening all along.

"Father Higgins has been arrested, haven't you read the papers?" Jane said angrily.

"Good riddance," said Ethel.

"Don't you start again," said Jane. "Where are these girls supposed to go, when everyone has turned their backs on them?"

"Anywhere but to see that pervert."

"That hasn't been proven yet."

"Not yet," Ethel said with finality.

In the breather that followed, the five minutes rang, and we all helped to make Tina look acceptable and to push her up the stairs. We had to push because she kept claiming to be quite incapable of performing in that emotional state. I told her that she had had a lucky escape because Mrs Huff hadn't shown up that night for her last-minute advice and notes.

In the wings, Greta was on the lookout for her friend whilst the other girls were already onstage. The first number was a schoolyard themed scene, "Remarkable Girl", an oldie from Ted Weems, with lots of hopscotching and rope jumping involved. This was supposed to be an amusing and light-hearted affair, but I suspected that Tina would struggle to smile all the way through the evening. Nevertheless, Greta grabbed her companion and dragged her forcefully across the stage to their position and put the skipping rope into her hand. The keen applause on the other side of the curtain grew fiercer. We heard the stage manager say "Positions, please". The rescue gang and I leaned against the theatre's cold wall and held out breath. But our worries were unfounded. As soon as the curtain rose, and the lamps were turned fully on, Tina and her group were as good as ever, jumping and giggling as if they didn't have a care in the world. I smiled at Little Mary standing in the semi darkness beside me. She looked relieved too. Ethel and Jane were having the same argument they had started in the dressing room and Rose was all eyes and ears, taking it in as it was her first week on the job. She was quite the professional and seemed to want to prove herself with Mrs Huff. Mary looked over to her and then back at me, all smiles. I nodded and raised my shoulders in puzzlement. I didn't remember ever being this nervous about this job. Mary's smile widened, and I was glad she was by my side in this odd setting.

Tina's outburst had unsettled me more than I admitted even to myself. It was a plight that loomed over every dancing's girl life. Some of us managed to make 'the mistake' with someone who was actually going to stand by us, like Helen probably. But most of us were recklessly playing the field, for reasons as diverse as money, glamour companionship or simply adventure. And, sooner or later, it resulted in Tina's plight. We then had various options to stay alive. None of them were pleasant, unless we very quickly found someone ready to settle down with us or the culprit was willing to pay without for having to settle down with us. Otherwise, there were always 'those women' who know how to get rid of the problem. Most of us chose that option, which was the only one that allowed us to keep working and be independent. If one survived the intervention, and that was far from certain, one could carry on one's life, more carefully. The other option was to keep it and be placed by a charitable institution, usually affiliated with a church of some denomination or other, as a maid until the baby was due. Depending on the circumstances, the girl could then keep it or give it up for adoption, which was the solution most of them chose.

The reason why a dancing girl was very unwilling to choose that last option was that it meant seven or eight months away from the stage and a figure that was mostly ruined. With a name everyone had forgotten and a body no one wanted onstage along the young beauties always available, their careers were mostly over and the majority of the girls didn't know any kind of trade except the one done laying on one's back. Hence a lot of us chose 'the women', no matter what the risk was.

Father Higgins had been helping girls for about ten years. I even had met him a few times before finding the Black Cat Theatre and sorting out my life. I remembered an intelligent white-haired man with piercing blue eyes and soft hands that he seemed to struggle to control or keep to himself. I had felt very uncomfortable around him and had avoided his company or help. But I had heard from other girls, especially younger ones, that he was a rather 'hands on' type of God worker. It had become customary to use his name to frighten girls into abstinence.

And now he had been arrested. Apparently one of 'his' girls had gone to the police to complain about his behaviour, something none of us had dared to do so far.

I was just about to smugly count myself lucky when the last notes of the other girls' number were playing and the curtain dropped. In a flurry of crushed costumes, exposed flesh and frantic scene changing, we took our places in our 'playground'. Our costumes were of the summer leisure variety, with less material and more sequins than regular girls on any playground. But we very much enjoyed this number. We had two swings which we got to use with abandon in order for our skirts to go flying. There was also a seesaw, again used with short skirts and many giggles. This whole scene took place in front of a painted backdrop of a park with blue sky. The end of our number and its song, "*The trouble with me is you*", always came too soon and we had to run backstage as the curtain touched the stage. The scene change was tremendous. They had to take the audience from a sunny day in the park into a lavish bedroom at night. In the meantime, we pretty much tore off our costumes. Then we draped ourselves in whatever silk or satin piece of cloth was ours for the tableau. As soon as they would let us, the other group having had to change during our number and waiting in the wings, all ten of us ran onstage and took our places on our revolve, draped ourselves on a sofa or struck our poses in our alcove.

As soon as Mrs Huff was happy with our set up, the curtain rose and the "*Penthouse Serenade*" filled the theatre with its dulcet tones. As usual, I had managed to obtain a reclining, if very nude, position and used this time to relax and bask in the admiration of the audience who got to see so much of me. But, as with all good things, and bad ones too, no matter what they say, it came to an end and, as soon as the curtain was closed, we ran backstage, so Ron and his crew could set up the seaside resort scenery.

In the meantime, the others got changed with lighting speed. There always was a bit of a competition between the stage hands and the girls, as to who would be ready first, the set or the performers. Mrs Huff was more than happy with that rivalry and usually the girls won. If they did, Ron or one of his boys would have a quip ready, something along the lines of, "You wouldn't want us to be finished too quickly, girls, right?" This didn't go down too well with the girls in question, waiting in the wings, but the show's timing didn't give them any time to respond.

After playing on a merry go round and jumping hoops, the audience watched Flora, Bridget, Norma, Greta and Tina frolic in prop waves and innocently toss the ball at each other. Again, Mrs Huff had selected a German song, "*Sommer, See und Sonnenschein*" to accommodate the taste of the sailors but also of the dignitaries and officers from the nation on the rise, who came to see our show often. We thought nothing of it and enjoyed the good times we had then.

Upon the last chord of the song, the curtain cut us off from the house lights and the girls came out of their last poses to go get changed of the curtain call. The crew came on to set up the park scenery for the last number. We had had a whole song to put on our evening frocks, complete with transparent frills and black lace. Upon their all clear signal, we ran on to take our place and the curtain rose. The song "*Pettin' in the park*" was played with languor by our in-house band. We strolled from tree to tree to the mellow beat of the music. The crowd's reaction was obviously more subdued than during a quicker, chirpier number but every now and then, we would dare a wink to the audience on the sly and get a hoot and applause, by name if the dancer was known to the men. That night young Rose had apparently something to prove because not only did she wink at the audience but lifted her long evening gown' skirt during a turn and gave the audience a good look at her firm derrière. Mrs Huff would probably have something to say about this kind of attention grabbing.

Once the moon had set on our nightly stroll through the trees, it was our turn to compete with the stage hands while the other girls had returned from the back of the theatre in their curtain call costumes and were waiting in the wings. This particular show's curtain call saw us reviving the "*Good Ship Lollipop*" costume, new ones having been made for the other group and adaptations been done to lucky Helen's costume to accommodate Rose slender figure. The crowd loudly let us know their approval of the 'all in red and white stripes' costume. Much to our approval, Mrs Huff had decided against also bringing the prop oversized lollipops.

Once we got back to the dressing room, the mood was positively ebullient, except for Tina who glumly took off her make-up and costume. Everyone else was chatting and laughing and swapping plans for the evening to come. As per usual, Mary kept to herself and quietly made herself ready as she was spoken for. But that night, Ethel was in a pugnacious mood, maybe the after effect of the argument with Jane. Whatever the reason, she shouted loudly across the dressing room.

"Hey Mary, I hear you recommended Father Higgins to help Tina with her little problem. Had a little problem of your own, did you?"

"Ethel, why don't you leave Mary alone and out of Tina's troubles?" I yelled so loud that not only did everyone hear, maybe even the audience, but the mood and chatter dropped to a Sunday morning mass murmur.

"What did you say?" Ethel hissed, getting up in piqued pride und underwear. "You don't get to tell me what to do, Lucy."

"Oh really?" I said, my eyes never leaving my reflection, applying rouge to my cheeks. "I think I just did."

"How dare you? Just because you're old

doesn't mean you get to boss us around."

"True. I am merely asking you not to pick a fight."

"You little…" Ethel said with a movement towards me.

"Stop it," Flora said calmly, holding her friend back. "You too, Lucy. Shut up, both of you."

"I have said my piece, I don't mean to add anything, unless Ethel wants me to."

"Lucy, stop! Ethel, please, sit down, get ready, we're leaving," Flora said, very calmly, guiding Ethel back to her chair and helping her with her hair.

They soon left and the mood became lighter, chatter resumed and plans for the night were hatched. Tina, as discreetly as she dared, came over to my make-up table. She was so demure that she nearly fit between the door frame of the stage steps and my mirror. She smiled shyly. I looked up and smiled back.

"Thank you, Lucy," Tina whispered.

"That's all right," I mock whispered back. "I know how upsetting that situation can be."

"Yes, it is," she whimpered. Then she silently sat on the second step of the stairs and started crying into her handkerchief. I sat down beside her, disregarding the fact that our behinds were entirely taking up the width of the stairs.

"I know, I know," I purred, patting her back.

"It's not just that…" she wailed.

"What else is the matter?" I asked, as much to get her talking, thus stopping the whimper, as to know what was going on under those lovely black tresses of hers.

"My brother," she stuttered through her tears. "He died."

"My goodness!" I said, not imagining her family's life to be half as dangerous as that. "How?"

"He… he," she began slowly, as if embarrassment was holding her back.

Her hesitation gave me the opportunity to look around. The dressing room was mostly empty, Flora and Ethel had been the first to leave. That robbed me of the possibility to ask Flora if Ethel had the same inclinations as she. That would've surprised me immensely, but my curiosity would have to wait. Or was it was simply *esprit de corps*?

The other girls had followed suit with Greta checking with me with a swift glance, as to whether her friend was all right. All who remained were Bridget, who had chosen that night to do something very elaborate with her hair, and Mary who, surprisingly, was faffing around with her things, as if she was trying to stay with a purpose other than to eavesdrop on our conversation. Darling Tina was oblivious to all of this, finally having mustered the courage to spill her beans.

"My brother was killed in a riot," she finally murmured.

"Really?" I said, beyond surprised. "Where? Why?"

"He works on the docks, at the port of Hamburg," she started before catching herself and chocking up again. "I mean, he worked at the docks, and he was a… a communist." She had said that last word so softly, I had to lean even closer to hear her. My ear brushed against her bangs, our knees were touching, and I am sure neither Mary nor Bridget had heard it.

"He was killed because he was a communist?" I asked in disbelief. I knew things were grim in Germany but surely, they hadn't deteriorated to the point of randomly killing good German dockers? No matter what their political convictions were.

"Yes! I mean, no! He was in a riot, because

he is a communist… because he is against the politics of the *National-Socialistische Deutsche Arbeiterspartei.*"

"Well, that's a mouthful!" I interrupted, trying to lighten the mood.

"Yes… and a lie," she said, not even slightly amused. "Because they are not there to help the workers, it's getting worse… and no one is doing anything to stop them, even the politicians are giving up… are giving him every right."

"You mean, Mr Hitler?"

"Yes, Mister Hitler," she said as if it was a laughable insult. "His SA were parading in Altona, between the train station and the… how do you say *Rathaus*, where the mayor works?"

"The townhall?" I offered.

"Yes, between the station and the townhall. You see, since the 16th June, SA and SS can walk in the uniforms again… and frighten people, and they are campaigning for the NSDAP to enter the Reichstag as a party… My brother joined a demonstration led by the SPD, the socialists… and two of the SA, the *Sturmabteilung*… the private police of the NSDAP, two of them were shot… so the police came in and shot all around." She started crying again. What a story. The Times definitely needed to report this. I briefly wondered why they hadn't and then I remembered that I didn't have time to read newspapers and no one in the dressing room reading them had said anything. But The Times very well might have said something.

"They even went into homes and shot people down from the roofs, sixteen dead... including my brother, I can't believe it!" she whimpered before wailing again.

And she was having a baby on top of that. I was surprised she hadn't tried to kill herself that night with a skipping rope or killed Ron for that matter. But I suppose she had been surrounded by people all evening and she had had enough death in her life so far, which probably meant that she was going to keep the baby. Mary must've come to the same conclusion because she had once again made her way to my make-up table undetected. She had waited there for a while until Tina had come to the end of her narrative.

"If you want, I can take you to St George's Church shelter tomorrow," she said softly. "Maybe you'll like it. Maybe they can help."

"Yes," Tina said, looking at Mary through her tears.

She got up and went to her table nearby to get ready. I walked Mary to her table to have a private conversation, behind the costume rail, because it might upset Tina.

"Do you think it's wise to leave her alone tonight?" I asked.

"I don't know," Mary said, looking at Tina in her mirror's reflection with concern. "You don't think she would... do something? Do you?"

"I don't know, she sounds really desperate."

"But, isn't she a catholic?"

"Yes, I believe so," I said not understanding the connection. "So?"

"Then she won't." Mary said with certainty. "Our religion forbids such a thing: it's a mortal sin."

"I see," I said, unimpressed.

Then I watched Tina get ready and thought about what Ethel had said about St George's Church and Father Higgins. I could feel a plan forming, along with a smile on my face. Both her situation and my new investigation would be helped by a little outing.

"I think I will come with you tomorrow, when you take Tina to the shelter."

"What? Why?" Mary said surprised and a

little suspicious.

"I haven't been to one of those places in a long time. It's good to remind oneself how dreadful it gets, just to stay on your toes about such things," I explained as offhandedly as I could.

Mary shushed me loudly. "Don't say such things. We don't want to frighten her." I had had my experiences with those places and Mary had visited many a lost soul, to bring soup and comfort.

"You're right. Let's keep that lovely surprise to ourselves," I sneered.

"You're impossible, Lucy," Mary said, quite mad. "You and I both want her to be all right, have her baby and get on with her life, right?"

"Sure, whatever life that will be."

"Do stop. She will be fine if she just accepts our help."

"And stays away from Father Higgins."

"She's too old for him," Mary snapped then clapped her mouth shut with both her hands.

"Well, that's nice," I said, amused by her reaction. "Isn't the girl who squealed on him at that shelter too?"

"She is," Mary said, glad to give a helpful

information, not knowing how that was settling the question of whether I was coming along to the shelter the next day.

I left Mary pondering about that and walked over to Tina. I crouched before her and put my hands on her knees, looking up at her in the glow of the make-up table mirrors lights.

"It's settled, Mary and I are taking you to a shelter where they can take care of you tomorrow. Will you come with us?"

"Of course, thank you, Lucy," she said, smiling at me and putting her hands on mine. I could see why Ron hadn't been able to keep his hands off her. She had thick black naturally curling hair and deep blue eyes and the softest skin. I just didn't understand what she saw in him. He was a bangers-and-mash English oaf. I still had to think of some way to avenge poor Tina and the cavalier way in which he had tossed her aside.

When we were all ready, Bridget had silently left a while back, probably wanting to stay out of our affairs, we waited on the curb for the cabs Maurice had gone to fetch for us. It was late, and the foot traffic had become much lighter. Also, the wind was nasty and had probably swept people off the streets.

Tina looked much better and seemed to be in better spirits. I really hoped she was going to show up at the appointed time the next morning. As we lived in various parts of London, we had decided to meet at the theatre and to walk to Bloomsbury. I think I had managed to worry Mary because she kept looking at Tina as if she might explode. I tried my best to soothe her with reassuring smiles, but her frown remained. After a while, Maurice came bouncing down our street with a cab in tow.

The next day, as we met Mary, Tina and I were surprised to find the plan had changed slightly. Mary had had a talk with her roommate and house mother. They had agreed that, given the circumstances, Tina had better go to the Salvation Army hospital, The Ivy House in Hackney. When I inquired as to what had brought about this decision, Mary started to squirm. Tina was happy to find help and not interested in questioning the reasons behind her benefactor's decisions. Mary hid behind some faith denomination incompatibilities, Bavarian Catholicism and Anglican church. When I pressed the matter a bit, quite unconvinced, she reluctantly admitted that it had to do with Tina's profession first and her country of origin second.

So that's how the wind was blowing in the religious circles. I sighed and shrugged and turned to hail a cab. Tina insisted on paying for the journey to Hackney. Mary and I laughed: we would only drive to King's Cross and then take the train to Hackney. That railroad trip already meant changing trains twice, so we indulged and took a cab to the station.

Hackney was even more provincial and quiet then I remembered. I found trees in parks, children playing in the streets, horse drawn carriages wherever you looked and peasants by the dozen. It was nigh eleven and I had plans for lunch, so I pressed our guide to show us the way. Mary seemed to know the way and I wondered how that could be. I made a mental note to ask her later.

We hurried down the muddy sidewalk and arrived soon at the feet of the impressive white gate, between two blocks of houses. It was an entrance large enough for a cab to fit through, probably to safeguard the identity of some of the more prominent patients in trouble. Suddenly, Tina, who had been a willing travelling companion so far, chatting and commenting the scenery as if we were going for a picnic, stood frozen, unable to move.

"We have to go in and announce you," Mary explained softly, trying to understand our friend's reluctance.

"I can't go," Tina said, staring at the tall façade and the bold letters on the white washed stone arch: Mother's Hospital.

"We are just having a look," I said, trying to be helpful. "If you don't like it, we'll go back. And anyway, you don't have that many choices, if you are set on keeping it."

"Yes!" Tina exclaimed, as if piqued in her Germanic pride. "Of course, I am keeping it."

"Fine, I am glad we cleared that up, again. Now on you go."

Mary and I nudged her slowly but steadily towards the admittance's door, inside the courtyard.

The rooms we found were very similar to the holding cells at the Yard. Unfortunately, I knew that from first-hand experience. The walls were white, the benches hard and the nurses' faces sullen. I am sure there were kind and smiling ones in this hospital, but I guess they kept them for those with less morally corrupt ailments. The instant I walked into that fallen women's purgatory, I was glad I didn't have to wait here with Mary and Tina as I had a plan to pursue. There were several women, bearing obvious signs of their 'fall' on the benches and I didn't like the looks they gave me. After they had been handed the form to fill out, I led Mary and Tina to some available spots at the end of a bench and told them I was going to look for a glass of water.

I suppose one wasn't supposed to roam in a hospital, but I was wearing one of my more discreet and respectable ensembles, the red lipstick might have given me away. So, after I wiped that off, I took the next best door to the right and started my inspection. I told myself I was doing it in part to give Tina a full report of what she was to expect. In reality, of course, I was looking for one specific patient. I wanted to help Barney with his investigation and, under the cover of being a good friend, I found myself in the hospital where the main witness was kept.

I too had perused the newspapers and had been disgusted by Father Higgins, the so-called 'Prostitute's Padre', and what he was accused of. Everyone knew that the 'news which made it into the papers' was but a small fraction of the truth. That's why, during what

I call my 'dark years', the police report only said I had been 'manhandled' when the constable had had to intervene. In this case, the papers had mentioned the well-meaning women's hospital, in Hackney, which had admitted the only girl who had told on Father Higgins: Barbara Scott. And there's only one hospital in Hackney that would take on such a girl in. Some secret.

So, there I was, exploring ward after ward, looking for Barbara. I didn't know her personally, but I was sure I would recognise her amongst the other fallen women. I wanted to find out first hand if all those stories were true. Some of her testimony seemed fanciful. Maybe she was blackening his otherwise spotless name out of revenge or attention grabbing. These girls, to which I belonged to, in principle, had very flexible notions of justice, fairness and the wrong being done. And she also had a reputation. Not in any way as sordid as Father Higgins but quite disreputable to be certain. The whole milieu knew that Father Higgins's activities with the girls, orphans, lost, on the streets mostly, balanced on a tremendously fine line, but no one had ever stepped forward to say he had crossed it. And that's why I was tiring myself out, tiptoeing around a hospital in the wrong part of town. I needed to find out why she had spoken up and all the others had kept quiet. There were, according to the papers, more than a thousand girls who had passed through the 'care' of Father Higgins.

Just as I was about to give up, I ventured in a less savoury ward, where the walls weren't white anymore but greenish and cracked, where the sheets hadn't been white in a long time and the smell was rather untoward. As soon as I pushed open the double doors, I knew I had decidedly nicer places to be and more charming people to visit. Those wards were full of ill women and not just recovering from having delivered babies they would never see again, crying a lot, but also dying from the pox or having their bowels eaten up by gin. But, of course, fate wouldn't let me get away with it quite so easily.

"What do you want?" said a coarse and powerful voice from one corner of the room. "You're no nurse."

"That's right," I said stepping in softly, gesturing to speak low, "I am not. I am looking for Barbara Scott."

"Who wants to know?" she barked.

She was dishevelled, her face slightly

smudged but I could tell that she would clean up nicely. She was probably testy because of the conditions she was living in. Looking around I admitted I would be an unpleasant wretch too, if I had to live here.

"My name is Lucy Turner. I am here to help her."

"You're not one of them journos," she inquired, frowning, "with their slippery questions?"

"No, I am not," I said, amused by her caution.

"So why are you here?" she asked gruffly.

"Are you Barbara Scott?" I asked, sitting down on her bed cautiously.

She was sitting cross legged on her cushion, her worn hands laying limply in her lap, her small breast obvious under the tattered shirt and her little white teeth shining under the grime of her hair. She was showing them to me awkwardly, by way of greeting.

"Yeah? So?"

"I am here to help you."

"I don't need no help. The coppers are watching out for me."

"I know. Some of them you can trust," I said, interrupting myself with an inflection and a tone that suggested just enough to get her worried. She jumped towards me like a doll on springs out of a box.

"What do you mean?"

"I just want your story to be told, even if," I whispered, "someone might try to," I sighed, "some people don't like to see the church dragged through the mud."

"Yeah, but everyone knows Higgins is a dirty old man."

"Yes, but that might not be enough," I insisted, "a young girl's word against that of a priest who has been redeeming girls for the past twelve years," I sighed, "if what you say is true and other girls step forward and say the same thing," I pretended to hesitate, "it'll mean that it was missed all this time, you see, and that will make them look bad. I am sure they won't like that." I put my hand on hers, as confidently as I could. "You don't have that many friends, Miss Scott, but I am one of them."

One might say that I was leading the witness, but it was truly because I had her best interest at heart. I am not entirely sure why because the creature was mostly repulsive to me, with her coarse hands grabbing my arm, her foul breath on my face and the stains on her hospital gown looking more mildewy with every passing minute. All the same, I was going to finish this.

"But I am telling the truth," she said squeezing my arm harder, her inflection on 'I' rather than 'truth' but I let it slide. I had to hear the whole thing before I made up my mind about her or her story or Higgins' wrongdoings.

"Well, let's see if you don't believe after you hear my story: I met Higgins a couple of years ago, I was 16 at the time. I met him on a street I liked to walk down on my walks," she looked at me as if I was supposed to understand something. "I had nowhere to go, you know. So I was just walking. And then he said I looked like a movie star. And he asked if he could have an autograph."

She paused and pushed the mop of dirty hair away from her face in a grand gesture. Then she looked at me as if even she didn't believe any of it.

"I know I am not much to look at now and I wasn't much better back then. I should've known. But I was hungry. And after I explained I wasn't there to pick up *clientele*, he asked if he could buy me lunch, because I looked hungry, he said. I was touched that someone would notice that about me. What a goose. We had lunch. And then again, the day after the following. And so on, for a few weeks. Then he asked if I had somewhere nice to live, I said that it was all right and he asked if he could see it," she sighed. "I saw no harm in it, so he visited me, you know, to talk, for a few weeks, again. After a while he gave me a bit of cash and he promised he would find work for me. I had no reason to doubt him," she sighed again. "One night, it was getting late. I told him I thought it would be best if he left, my landlady isn't too happy about gents staying the night, you see," she said, very much the righteous girl, although I had no illusions as to how she got her money at the time she met the louse. "He said he wanted to protect me because he didn't like the types that were roaming the digs. The nerves on that bloke, right? He stayed from time to time. At first, he kept to the chair. But after a few nights, he did not. And when I said no," her voice trailed off, looking at me half disgusted, half amused, "he'd relieve himself, alone."

I wasn't born into this *milieu* but I had been forced to live in it for long enough not to be shocked by such behaviour, but I couldn't help being struck dumb. I couldn't believe the baseness of that man, prying on not so innocent but definitely vulnerable girls. I also found her calm and amused expression confounding. She recounted it all as if was some gossip from the papers. I felt quite queasy and somewhat regretted having come all this way for someone who seemed to have suffered very little from the ordeal. Then again, I was here now and she wasn't letting me go without a few more sordid details for the road.

"He was keen as mustard, you see. And other girls in the house, and in other houses, they all said they had to fight him off. Some of them didn't dare to and, well, got what they had comin'," she said, almost pitying them.

"He had his way with them? With girls you know?" I asked

"Yes, he tried it with my mate, Anna, from next door. But she's a brunette. So when she said no, he didn't stick around too much."

"Thank you, Barbara," I said, getting up, quite ready to leave.

"You goin'?" she asked pleadingly.

"Yes, I am surprised no one has found me yet to kick me out," I said, looking desperately around for someone with authority, but no one cared.

"Sometimes, they don't come for days,"

she confirmed.

"My friends will be wondering where I am. I really have to go."

"Will you come back?"

"Of course," I said, trying to sound convincing while looking at the squalor around me.

"I need a friend," she said.

She looked almost endearing, with her eyes made larger by hunger, the shadows under her eyes and the parched lips. I wish there was something more I could've done but I was at the end of my self-restraint and had heard one too many of the women in this room throwing up, barely making it over the side of their bed. I was either going to throw up too or faint or both. So, I promised to do everything I could to seal Higgins' fate and help her out.

I practically ran all the way back to the entrance hall. The pregnant girls had been replaced by new ones on the benches of the waiting area and my friends greeted me with worried looks.

"Are you all right, Luce?" asked the fresh-faced Mary.

"Yes, we were looking for you," said Tina.

"Yes, I am all right," I smiled. "Let's go,"

I pressed them on.

Pretty soon we were on Hackney's train station platform, waiting for the train that would rescue me from the ward's dank smell and the clammy air that seemed to follow me around. I didn't want to alarm my friends or have to tell them where I had been, so I put on a brave face and smiled a lot.

It was only when we got off the train at King's Cross that I remembered that the meal I was to eat before this night's show was going to be a challenge too.

What a day.

I said good bye to my friends without much of a fuss since we were going to see each other in a few hours. On the way home, as well as deciding what to wear, I thought about my promise to Barbara. I would have to talk it over with Barnaby and convince him to go visit the priest in the morning. He was to be found at his parish because, since Barbara's accusations, he had been released from prison but remained under investigation.

At five, I had just managed to get dressed and made up after my restoring nap when there was the familiar knock on the door. Barnaby didn't take off his coat or hat since he said he had a cab waiting downstairs. In a whirlwind, I grabbed my hat, my coat, my purse and off we went to Fulham Road. Barney's aunt and uncle, having heard that we hadn't celebrated my birthday, invited us exactly a month later, into their home, for a hearty meal, as she had put it, he said. His relation to his aunt and uncle was a bit confusing to me but I supposed I would get more information that night. Little did I know what a wretched ordeal that was going to be.

I got my first foul foreboding the moment Auntie Kate opened the door and I started feeling unwell. It was a very respectable house, white washed with a black iron fence. No front garden but immaculately clean. What irritated me from the get-go was her overly cheerful welcome phrase.

"Barnaby, you're a sight for sore eyes," she said, staring at him all the while.

Barney had literally to push me into her line of sight for her to acknowledge my presence.

"And you brought your friend. How do you do, dear?" she said, again the sounds kind enough but the eyes dead as a stuffed tiger.

"I told you I was going to bring her, auntie," he said, pushing past her and walking in, keeping me in front of him. "You

36

remember? It's Luce's birthday."

"Yes, of course, I remember," she said unimpressed. "We will do our best to entertain you, Bernard!" she squealed up the stairs. "Barnaby and his friend are here!"

"Her name is Lucy," Barney said with a hint of impatience.

"Of course," Kate said, before putting her arm around my shoulders and guiding me to the sitting room, her hand an iron vice. "So, tell me, what do you do? How did you two meet? When will you get married?"

She guided me to a settee and practically pushed me down. Barney sat beside me, although there was hardly enough room for two. He took my hand, letting me know he had noticed how unsettled I was by his aunt's behaviour and radically nosy questions. If I didn't know any better, I would've guessed that she had picked those that would make me most uncomfortable.

"Auntie Kate, come on. You are drilling her with questions. Could we have a drink first?"

"Of course, where are my manners?" she said, laughing forcedly. "Sherry all right?" she asked before vanishing into the kitchen.

"Sure," I whispered, trying to make myself

invisible.

"She means well," he whispered back. "She's just very protective of me."

I looked up at him searching his serene features for a trace of irony. I only found warmth and kindness. I fell in love with him all over again.

"You're actually the first girl I ever brought here, so she's a bit…"

"What? You never brought anyone else?"

"No," he smiled. "What kind of a man do you take me for?"

"I don't know," I hesitated. "But I wasn't your first… woman, was I?"

"No," again that smile. "There were a few others. Very few. And not the type I wanted to meet my aunt."

"I see," is all I had time to say before she stood in front of us again.

"Drinks all 'round," she said giddily.

She handed us the cut glass tumblers with the smallest serving imaginable, she put her head towards the stairs and literally hollered.

"Bernard dear, it is time for you to come down. Our guests have arrived."

Barney looked at me and winked, which managed to make me smile. I suppose he was quite used to the games she played but they were all new to me and I struggled to remain affable.

"I don't know what is keeping that man," she said with a forced smile, sitting down with her almost empty glass at the opposite end of the impeccably kept room. "We both are so happy to meet you. We so seldom get to see Barnaby. And now he has a friend. Please tell me, if it's not too drilling. Lucy, what do you do?"

I was unsure how to respond. Barney and I hadn't discussed the lies for this meal, which was a mistake. I had a standard lie I used for any occasion where I knew that the word 'cabaret dancer' would do me disservice. But now Barney was here, and I didn't know what he had told her. I didn't want to be caught out in any way by this woman who was transforming into a dragon before my very eyes. Taking my time to smile at Barney, I tried to read his thoughts. Since he didn't pick up the hint, I just went with the standard lie.

"I am a dancer at the Royal Opera House, in the chorus of their ballet company of course. I am just part of the scenery really."

"I see," she said as if I had admitted to selling secret submarine plans to Jerry. "And how did you ever meet a ballet dancer,

Barnaby?"

"You know how I am, always chasing ruffians around Covent Garden. One day I ran past the stage door and Lucy was just coming out. We bumped into each other."

I had to tip my hat to him. I mean, I had always admired his intelligence but the speed at which he had spun such a credible fib was impressive. Of course, the truth was a lot less honourable or romantic. I had been dancing for a month at some dingy watering hole. It was close enough to the Aldwych to be frequented by honourable gents but lowly enough to pay us meagre wages and let us bring our own costumes. It came as no real surprise when Barney and his colleagues raided the place one night. I had only been on the streets and trying to survive by 'dancing' for about a year, but I knew these places and how they ended up 'closed for business'. He had been so green and new to this world, cute in the most charming way. I immediately fell for him as he pushed me to the streets and into the police van, cautiously as only a first timer would. All the girls noticed the young bobby and we talked and sniggered about him all the way to the Yard.

I must've been day dreaming because

when I looked up, I saw a burly man, with dull eyes behind thick glasses, wearing an even duller brown cardigan. He was holding his hand stretched out to me like a doll.

"Lucy? Are you awake?" Barney asked nicely, nudging me a little. "This is Uncle Bernard."

"Very nice to meet you," I said half rising.

"No need to get up, dear," Kate said harshly. "Now, Bernie, sit yourself down in your chair, so we can talk to this poor girl."

"Yes, dear," he muttered as he sat on a large armchair. He seemed to relax a little, as if the deep cushions were soon going to swallow him up and he wouldn't be called up to partake in the conversation. I also noticed that no one bothered to serve him a drink.

"He has taken the pledge," Kate said, as she noticed my looking at Bernard's empty hands. "When he's thirsty, he'll get some water from the kitchen. Won't you, dear?" she said, as smarmy as they come.

"Yes, dear," said the round-shouldered man vanishing into his armchair.

"So, dear Lucy, what are you appearing in right now?" asked Kate with an inquisitive gaze.

For a moment, I thought I would have to

come up with a very good excuse not to be appearing. I wasn't going to pull a ballet or an opera out of thin air without knowing if she followed the program of the Royal Opera House. She seemed the cultural type. But Barnaby cut in, all smiles.

"Come on, Auntie Kate, leave Lucy in peace. Wasn't there going to be some supper?"

"That's right," she said, getting up and ushering us into the dining room where the table had been set in a Spartan manner, with a dreadful porcelain statue in lieu of a fresh flowers centrepiece. "You have places to go. Far be it from me to make you late. Please, take a seat," she said, ever the considerate hostess. "No dear, that's Bernard's chair. You're sat here."

As I confusedly got up, she designated a chair between herself and Bernard. Hence, I had the joy to stare at Barnaby's reassuring face all through the meal.

Thank God.

Auntie Kate vanished into the kitchen while we sat in silence under the very white light of the three-armed brass chandelier. A huge clock ticked against one wall, large blooms glared at us from the Morris wallpaper and dusk was settling over the back garden. I suddenly longed to be far, far away. Had Barnaby not seen the evening going this way? He appeared mostly amused by the whole charade. Or did he have such a filial obligation towards them that he agreed to go through the motions for the sake of propriety? He had never told me about them before a few weeks back. Or was it some kind of test for me, to see if I'd hold my end up in such a sticky situation? He knew how brave, enduring but also sensitive I was. Because I have to admit this situation was taking its toll on me. And I had a show to perform after that. Then my gaze fell on Bernard. Was he her prisoner, unable to look after himself?

Barney must have been watching the direction my eyes took because he addressed himself with the richest, softest tone to the old man.

"And you, Uncle Bernard, how are you?"

"I am fine, my dear boy," Bernard said after being startled to be addressed and apparently lost in thought. "How are you?"

"I am fine, Uncle Bernard. Have you met my friend Lucy?"

"Hello Lucy," his foggy and vacant gaze fell on me. "I am Bernard. How nice to meet you."

He shook my hand. I was quite lost. Kate practically barged into the dining room with oven mitts around a piping hot pot.

"Bernard, you met Lucy earlier, in the living room, don't you remember?" she asked with a definite tone of menace in the latter question.

"Yes, of course, dear," he said looking at her raised eyebrows then at the pot she had demonstratively dropped on the heat pads in the middle of the table. "What's for dinner?"

"Silly man: always after the food," she said as she sat down back in the gracious hostess mode, taking off her mitts. "Meat loaf, potatoes and carrots," she said as she proudly opened the lid.

"It smells delicious," Barney lied. I smiled in accord.

The loaf looked like it had been scraped up from the bottom of a coal cellar, the potatoes were strangely gelatinous and the carrots were decidedly wrinkled. To top it off, the contents of that pot smelled like they had been sitting in a cold oven for a week and warmed up just for us. I started planning how I was going to make it look like I'd eaten my share. Sadly, there was no dog to be fed in this house. Then again, I don't think I wished any living creature the curse of having to live in this house. I was getting quite upset because I had a show to dance through and I couldn't take a queasy stomach. I pleaded with Barnaby with a look, but he just kept smiling as if it was some kind of circus show. As it turns out, I wouldn't have had to worry. No food was ever to touch my plate, let alone my lips.

It all unravelled rather quickly.

"I heard you say that Lucy is your friend, Barnaby dear."

"That's right," he said, his smile growing a little more nervous.

"But surely it's more that that," she said, a knife in her hand.

"How do you mean?" Barney said, his mood darkening ever so slightly.

"You've never brought anyone home before. Are we to understand that she is a sleeping partner in a venture of yours?"

I mightily struggled not to laugh at the choice of words.

"I have no ventures, Auntie Kate," Barney said sternly. "I am a detective with Scotland Yard, as well you know. And no, she isn't a sleeping partner but my lover. Is this what you wanted to hear?"

"Not particularly but I suppose it can't be helped," she said looking at me disdainfully. "And what about her employ? Are you really going to try and make me believe she's a ballet dancer?"

By then, Bernard and I had entirely disappeared from their scope of awareness. Years of tensions were being chewed over and no one else mattered.

"No, 'Auntie' Kate, she isn't with a ballet company. She is a dancer but in a revue at the Black Cat Theatre."

"I have heard of the place. Is it the kind of girls you consort with these days? You could have done so much better. I mean, look at her.

"Auntie Kate," Barnaby hissed, getting up. "Not another word out of you. I don't need your blessing, we don't need your blessing," he said, pulling me out of my chair. "I love this girl and if you want to see what she can do, which is just as difficult as any ballet dancer without the air of sanctity, come to the theatre whenever you want. You can meet me at eight any night and I'll buy your tickets."

He stormed out of the room, pushing me ahead of him. "You said you know where it is," he added over his shoulder.

We threw on our coats in the hall in utter

silence.

"And enjoy your meat loaf," he hollered before closing the front door on us.

We walked the nerves off in silence for a while. Then, as I am not too keen on silence, especially with Barnaby in the state I was seeing him in for the first time, I started a random conversation.

"Have you heard Herbert Hoover is not going to attend the Olympic Games in Los Angeles?"

"That'll teach him to call the crisis his country is going through a 'Great Depression'. Nobody has the heart to compete," he replied non-committal, staring at the road crossing ahead.

"Apparently there's only going to be half the participants at the games."

"Of course, who can afford the trip or the expenses in this day and age?"

"What I cannot understand is that Germany is turning in a bad way and the press still insists that those games are the most important thing right now."

"I suppose it's everyone for themselves these days," he said bitterly as we waited to cross the road.

"That's not strictly true. You really stood

up for me tonight, thank you."

"I wasn't going to let her be rude to you, was I?" he said, turning to me and putting his arms around my waist.

"But why did we go there in the first place?"

"I don't truly know," he sighed. "I suppose I wanted to check whether my memories were tainted by my childish perception of things or if she was the inconsiderate woman I remembered."

"She certainly seems to like you."

"It makes the whole thing worse. Her affections have made me uncomfortable for the longest time."

"Do you think they will actually show up for the show?"

"Maybe," he smiled.

"When they do, it'll be an entertaining evening, to be sure," I laughed and kissed him.

I am quite sure that Barnaby, and the rest of the metropolitan police for that matter, would have disapproved of my visit to St George's Church. As a matter of a fact, he very much did, as the story will show.

But the suspect in this little adventure

sounded more and more interesting and I had to meet him alone, at least for a while. Now, I thoroughly disapproved of anyone who took advantage of a girl's misery. Having said that, Barbara hadn't appeared miserable or disheartened. Actually, in the midst of all that illness and dying, she had seemed positively radiant. Her present situation seemed to her, but mostly to me, much worse now that she wasn't under Father Higgins' 'protection' anymore.

To me there was room for doubt and I wanted to hear it from the horse's mouth. And after the dinner two nights ago, I thought Father Higgins might actually be charming company. Little did I know that I was about to meet one of the more intriguing villains I was ever to come across. I had accumulated nasty encounters over the years, be it professionally or in helping justice be rendered, but he was a law unto himself.

It had started rather normally, a muggy summer's day in London, a crowded street, roaring traffic on Regent Street and the excitement of doing something not quite legal. Maybe I could help Barney's investigation in the process. I was walking with a spring in my step, my umbrella whooshing at my side, heading for Hanover Square.

I was aware that it was madness to go and see Father Higgins, but I needed to look that man in the eye and hear him say these lies to my face. The danger that might lay in wait for me there was only making this outing more exciting. The fact that he might tell me something new was secondary.

I knew the shelter well, many of my friends had to stay there at one time or another. Most girls lived in fear of having to go there. No one went freely, only out of sheer necessity. I was plucky enough to have kept out of it but I visited many poor souls who had been, according to their soon-to-be-gone beaux, 'careless'. I had had words with many of them and maybe I was the reason why some of them left. Then again, I was definitely the reason why a few of them stayed and stood by their pregnant girlfriends. I just couldn't stand how callous some of those men were with girls who had come into that 'situation' for all intents and purposes because of them. For a dancing girl, an unwanted pregnancy usually meant the end of crazy nights and the beginning of factory work. At the rate politics were degrading in Europe, there was going to be plenty of work for them. From what I saw, the girls were being free with their charms.

I arrived on the steps of St George's Church on familiar ground. I knew that the shelter's entrance was to the side. It was safe to assume that the Colonel Blimps of this world didn't want fallen girls going to the shelter through the church's holy front doors. I knocked on the white door with the small window and entered. I had made that decision because there was something of a racket going on and I wasn't sure anyone would hear me knocking any time soon.

Upon entering, I inferred that the mellow weather we'd been having had led to much dallying in the parks because there were at least a dozen girls coming and going, arguing and shouting, mostly making a nuisance of themselves. They were all quite pregnant with hair stuck to their foreheads from perspiration. I was far too amused by their clucking and bickering to interrupt them by coughing. In the end, however, one of them noticed me.

"Miss!" she squealed. "There's another one!"

Before I could protest my health, a lovely grey-haired lady appeared in the white door frame and came towards me with a redeeming angel's look on her face. I wish Barney's aunt would've been so much more like her. She was almost overwhelmed and tried to keep up propriety in spite of the mayhem around her.

"Hello, I am Miss Cunningham," she crooned. "Can I help you, dear?" she asked, her calm demeanour contrasting sharply with the chaotic atmosphere in the building.

"Yes, thank you," I started and then caught myself. "It's not what you think," I added quickly.

"Of course, I can see you're a wise girl," she said kindly.

I was never to find out on what clue she had based that opinion because the noise had reached a new height and it showed no sign of abating. Time became of the essence.

"I am here to see Father Higgins," I said as loudly as I could without shouting.

"Of course," she replied, assuming I was getting married. "He is in the vestry, preparing his next sermon," she said, pointing me towards a door to the right.

I was relieved when I was finally able to lean against the other side of that door, having encapsulated the chaos away from me. I could hear the old lady's soft voice making peculiar,

A man with short grey hair sat at the table with his back to the door.

appeasing sounds whilst the harpies kept arguing.

After I had resumed my spirits, I walked down the white corridor with the old creaking floorboards letting everyone within hearing distance know I was coming. For a second, I was horribly reminded of my last visit to a deserted church and its deadly consequences. I firmly shook the memory out of my head and soon found an open door to my left.

It was the vestry Miss Cunningham had told me about, a midsized room with a desk, two worn armchairs and a serving table. One wall was full of shelves holding books and religious imagery. Blue skies brought soft light through high windows opposite. A man with short grey hair sat at the table with his back to the door. He seemed to be leaning over an old book. He was definitely writing with dedication because I could hear his fountain pen scratching the paper furiously. He was so consumed by writing that he gave no sign of having heard me come in. I took a few careful steps to the side, towards the couch, hoping to sit down while I waited for him to be done. He was wearing black trousers and a black short sleeved shirt with the customary white collar. The clothes were tight enough to reveal a sinewy body and an energetic persona. When I came close to sitting down, he put down the pen and closed the book, turning to me as if he knew who I was, a sharp eye looking me over.

"Hello," he said, with such a tone, I wondered whether he could read my mind and knew why I was there.

"Hello," I said, trying to remain as unimpressed as possible.

But he studied me with such overt attention and, dare I say, pleasure that I couldn't help blushing and stuttering.

"I am sorry, I didn't mean to."

I was confused by his manner, a state of mind that kept with me throughout our conversation. I was on my toes all the time I was there, never knowing what madness might come next. He made perfect sense when he talked but his gaze made him look like he was capable of anything. He reminded me of a creature I had seen at the Natural History Museum. What was I doing there? What is a girl to do when her man is out of town for a few rainy days? It was labelled 'Iguanodon' and though only the skeleton was on display, the drawing showed a fierce creature with a smile of small white sharp teeth, a head of spines and a set of long lethal claws at the end of thin, scaled limbs. While this man had a regular head of white hair, the rest of the description fitted him quite well. His little pointed teeth often flashed in a seemingly warm smile and his thin fingers gave the impression of possessing a life of their own.

"How may I help you?" he said, as if he was a salesman at Selfridges.

"I was wondering if I could ask you a few questions?" I said, less and less sure about this visit.

"I suppose, seeing how you are not one of our residents and you seem to be keener than most," he said, getting up, "you want to talk about that girl's accusations."

He was about my height but the intensity of his gaze and charisma made him appear larger.

"I went to see her yesterday and…"

"Really? You saw her?" he said, genuinely interested.

"Yes," I said, uncertain what the reply should be to keep him happy.

"They won't let me into that wretched hospital, women only and all that. Since the papers have published her tale, I too wanted an explanation," he said. He seemed to think it was all a rather silly misunderstanding. "And how is the dear girl? I hear the premises are rather ghastly?"

"Yes, they are, how may I say, not very nice. It certainly isn't the Ritz," I said, trying to keep the mood light, still feeling very troubled, without being able to say why.

"No," he said kindly. "I imagine it isn't. How is she? Has she asked about me?"

I was unable to prevent my eyebrows rising slightly. He noticed.

"You seem surprised. Did she tell you everything? Was it that nasty?" he asked, moving ever so slightly towards me. "All very ugly?"

"Not all of it," I said lightly, as if I hadn't noticed the air of menace that had crept into his demeanour. "She said that, at first, you were kind, that's why she trusted you, you know, to come in and visit her at her lodgings and to stay the night."

He stopped moving, as if trying to guess my opinion of him. His eyes were two slits and I could feel some kind of emanation coming from him. My heart picked up the pace.

"I am sorry, where are my manners?

Would you like some tea?" he asked, changing the subject and his behaviour so completely in a moment that I was quite speechless. He pointed to the two faded rose Georgian wing armchairs and a low table.

"Mrs Cunningham will be along any moment to ask whether you want some as well." He paused, still watching me closely, then smiled, as if he noticed my discomfort. "I recommend you accept her proposition. It will make our conversation so much more pleasant."

"Then I must accept," I said, still smiling, finding it hard to conceal my trepidation.

How ignorant could any girl be to let such a man stay in her room for the night? Every inch of his wiry body seemed to ooze some foul liquid that threatened to choke me even as he moved away. He casually sat down in an armchair and smiled as if he was posing for a photographer. I silently thanked whoever hadn't put a couch in the vestry but two distinct armchairs, separated by the insurmountable barrier of a cabriole legged table. Or so I sincerely hoped. An instant after I had sat down, the slender figure of Mrs Cunningham stood in the door, asking about tea and biscuits.

"Look at that," she marvelled, "he always knows when I'll be coming by, waiting like a faithful dog in his chair. Oh, I am sorry, father, I didn't mean…"

"Don't worry, Mrs Cunningham," he said kindly to the blushing old lady. "And you're right, I know when you are about to visit me. I assure you, I look forward to it every day. Who was it who said, 'We are what we repeatedly do. Excellence, then, is not an act, but a habit'?"

"I don't know, Father, but it is wonderfully said," she said, beaming.

"Isn't it just? Well, dear Mrs Cunningham, I'll have some tea, thank you."

"And you, Miss?" she asked, not entirely inviting.

"Yes, I think I have quite convinced her," he said, giving me a wink that turned my spine to ice and my stomach to a sewer.

"Of course, Father Higgins has a knack for converting lost girls," she said approvingly, apparently blind to any of the newspaper reports. "I will be right back with your tea."

"And biscuits!" he hollered, as a joke.

"We'll see," she called back, chuckling a little.

"Such a charming lady, so helpful and

devoted," he said. "Now, what did Barbara have to say?"

I stammered, still dumbfounded by the contrast between what Barbara and the papers had made him out to be and what I saw with my own eyes. After a deep breath, I regained the command of my vocabulary.

"Not much," I grinned. "She's in shock, you see. That's why I came to you. I want to get a more coherent story."

"Why do you have such an interest? Are you one of Barbara's friends? You're not with the police, are you?" he asked, all smiles as he had made an amusing joke.

"No, I am, yes, a friend of Barbara's. She has confided in me and wants me to testify as to her character," I said, letting on that her character wasn't all that recommendable. "Having said that, I'd like to hear both stories before I pick sides."

"Wise girl," he said, like a proud teacher.

"Father Higgins, how would you describe your relationship with Barbara?"

"My goodness, are you sure you're not with the police? You certainly sound like them," he said, sniggering like a schoolboy then catching himself. "I didn't have a relationship per say with Barbara. I met her occasionally in a tea house, at first."

"But very soon, you were shown into her rooms?"

"Yes, upon her insistence. She was happy to take my money, my advice and my care. Although I didn't see a great improvement in her."

"Poor lamb," Mrs Cunningham said, setting down the tray on the elegant table.

"How do you mean?" I asked, surprised at that woman's blind trust.

"You are talking about Barbara, aren't you?" she asked, seeking Father Higgins' approval to voice her opinion. He nodded.

"You've met her?" I asked.

"Of course, I meet all the girls Father Higgins takes under his wing. Goodness knows there are enough fallen girls and orphans roaming the streets of London. But the ones who really want to be saved always find their way here."

She glanced almost amorously towards Father Higgins. She seemed blissfully ignorant of the facts surrounding his preference for younger, slower, fresher, fairer and healthier lost girls than the dark, strong and sharp one sitting across from him.

"Thank you, Mrs Cunningham," he said, as

much to thank her as to subtly ask her to leave. I assumed it meant that he wanted to tell me things that a saintly old lady should not hear.

"I really must be going," she said on cue. "I'll be back later for the tray."

"Thank you, Mrs Cunningham," I said, as much to thank her as to subtly ask her to come back soon. I wasn't quite sure my suggestion would come across as clearly.

"So, you were trying to improve Barbara or her condition, at least?" I asked as I watched him busy himself with serving tea.

"Both, I hoped," he sighed, "but she wasn't very cooperative."

I was so glad to not yet have my cup and saucer in my hands or they would surely have crashed on the floor upon hearing those words, a little too open to interpretation. Considering what Barbara claimed he had tried to make her do, I wasn't surprised he resented her for being uncooperative. Where I was mystified was the offhand way in which he talked about it, as if she had been a reluctant scholar. Again, he must have been aiming for the double entendre that troubled me because he handed me a cup of tea with the most winsome smile, as if shocking me had been his aim all along. Maybe he was trying to frighten me away without uttering a single threat. They would come later, no doubt. I was itching to let him know in so many words that he had met his match and that I had met far more repugnant characters in my time. Having said that, none had been so sickeningly sweet and fiendish. But that would ruin my plan. I wanted to see his predatory side when faced with an innocent lamb. I led him on.

"What makes you think she wasn't improving?" I asked, slowly sipping my weak tea, eyeing the biscuit with caution.

"For one thing, she kept company with the worst ruffians in spite of my entreaties to seek more educated and genteel people. She kept saying that those people bored her, and she didn't understand half of what they said."

"Other than money, how did you help her?"

"I gave her lessons in deportment and tried to improve her oral skills." I shuddered again but he kept going as if he was talking about the weather. "But she was a stubborn girl."

"She *is* still alive," I said.

"Yes, of course, I meant that she was a difficult student with me, at the time."

Quite out of the blue, very much how I

must have appeared earlier, suddenly Barnaby stood in the door to the vestry. How he had managed to walk silently down that corridor was a mystery. I am not quite sure to whom he gave a darker look, Father Higgins or myself. I guessed that my lovely man had his suspicions about the pious Father and he wasn't happy that I was talking to him. Alone.

"Hello Inspector," Father Higgins greeted him. He sounded like he was welcoming an old friend. "Please take a seat. We are having tea and I am sure Mrs Cunningham can provide us with another cup and a fresh pot."

"Thank you, Father Higgins. I was going to ask you a few more questions but Lucy has already taken up far too much of your time," Barney growled, his eyes burning reproachfully into mine.

"Not at all. Your charming friend was only asking me questions after visiting Miss Scott, to check her facts, as it were."

"She visited her?" Barney said, winding even tighter, not looking at me purposefully, just moving slowly in my direction.

"Yes," the priest said, staring at Barney and I alternatively, trying to grasp the situation. "Young lady, you shouldn't have done that, apparently," he chuckled. "Don't worry, Inspector, I haven't told her anything I haven't told you and your colleagues already."

"I certainly hope so," he said. "Come on Lucy, let's go."

"But I wasn't," I protested as he practically pulled me out of my armchair.

"Yes, you were," he said, making for the door, still not looking at me. "Good bye, Father Higgins."

"Bye bye lovers," I heard him call after us.

I didn't understand Barney's aggravated behaviour. Surely, I wasn't in any danger in a vestry in the middle of London in the middle of the day. Soon however, I grasped why he over-reacted the way he did. In the cab taking us to the theatre, he explained himself. Once he got a word in.

"What is the matter with you?" I said, half joking, half chiding. "You barged in there as if he was manhandling me."

"Maybe I should've waited a little longer," he sneered.

"You really think that that was coming?" I asked, surprised.

"I don't know," he said, deep in thought. "Don't you ever get tired of it?"

"Tired of what?" I asked, laughing.

"Putting yourself in the way of danger?" he said, staring at me with a look that made me choke.

"No, I don't get tired of it," I said, haughtily. "I intend to do so as long as I can take it. Barney, I am sure he's not that dangerous. I know the…"

"No, you don't," he said as he leant towards me as if admitting some terrible secret. "Another girl has come forward. And she wasn't as resourceful as Miss Scott to protect her virtue."

"He abused her?" I asked, feeling my stomach turn.

"Yes, Lucy, that is why I went to see him and why I was rather upset to find you with him, alone, playing your little 'I just have a few questions' game with him. The man is a fiend, Luce. You have to stay away from him."

"I will," I replied. "As opposed to what you seem to think, I don't like thieves, scoundrels, murderers or rapists. The only reason I help you is so they get their come-uppance and that a few girls might survive with their virtue intact."

I started crying, feeling tired from the fear the priest had instilled in me and for the poor girl who hadn't a boyfriend to get her out of trouble. Barnaby was embarrassed by my tears and took me into his arms.

"I am sorry, Luce. I pushed you too hard."

"No, no, it's all right," I said looking up at him. "I am the fool who thinks she can make a difference when all I do is put myself in situations you have to bail me out of."

"No, that's not true," he appeased me. "All right, maybe, sometimes. But at least we get to see each other every time you do."

I laughed, and he joined in. We enjoyed a moment's silence while the cab rocked us gently through the city.

"You don't know how lucky you are," he sighed.

"To have a bloke like you to snatch me away from predators in the nick of time?"

"That too," he said softly. "I meant that you are lucky to be onstage tonight."

"Why?" I asked, searching his face.

"Tonight's the night Auntie Kate and Uncle Bernard are coming to see the show."

"What? She took you up on your offer?"

"Exactly! I am sure Bernard manages to sneak off for some fun now and then, but I never thought she would agree to it."

"And what did you say?"

"What was I going to say? I got us three tickets."

"That strange woman is going to see me starkers?"

The expression made Barnaby laugh.

The cab stopped in front of the stage door, Maurice already looking out for me. We stepped off and Barney paid the driver.

"Rather annoying, I know, but I got over it. I am sure she will, too."

"Barney, I am not sure I will."

Maurice, who had been giving me discreet signs to hurry up and enter, now approached.

"I am so sorry *mademoiselle*, but you are very late, you have to come in now."

"Yes, I know, I am coming. What are we going to do?" I asked Barney.

"You go to your rehearsal, dance your heart out tonight and be sure to join us in the audience afterwards for some champagne."

"Barney, you won't…"

"Milk the situation for all it's worth? I can't wait to see her reaction, it'll be priceless, but remember, after the show, you come to me, no sneaking away, you'll be the fallen woman she expects and make me proud."

"All right," I said, and kissed him.

Maurice tugged at my sleeve. I turned

around, giddy as can be and planted a big, fat kiss on the cheek of the French *célibataire*. I heard Barnaby laughing as I ran down the corridor, towards our dressing room.

I had quite lost track of time and Mrs Bartlett and the girls were rehearsing when I snuck in. My lateness having become the norm, Mrs Bartlett only rolled her eyes at me and called the number and dance we were rehearsing.

For the first time in years, I was nervous to go onstage. I had a small knot in my stomach and it was hard to smile. Some of the girls remarked on it but my lack of a feisty response got them worried. I meticulously put on my make-up like I was auditioning at the Opera House. I slipped into my far too revealing summer dress with my skin crawling and wondered how Barnaby was faring at the other end of this building.

Later that evening, he told me how things went when we met at his place to lick our wounds, and, since we were at it, the rest of our tired bodies too.

"Lucy, I hope you had a good time tonight because mine was as bad as I had anticipated. On the one hand, I was looking forward to see Auntie Kate and Bernard squirm as they watched you and your friends get their kit off. On the other, I knew she would do everything she could to make us uncomfortable. Turns out, she had outdone herself in bringing along the foulest of moods. When I asked her why she'd come, because she obviously didn't want to be there, she said Bernard had insisted. What a joke. And Bernard was quick to respond, if very quietly but with a raised eyebrow, 'I didn't say a thing'. If the old boy hadn't looked so frightened, it would've been hilarious. She rallied and said that since they'd come all this way and I had bought the tickets, they might as well watch the show. Bernard didn't give any sign whether he had a preference but followed her, very much the lap dog he has become. I think their relationship took a turn for the worse when I left to live on my own. I don't know why. He hasn't always been like that. When I was little, he was fun, and we would go to the park to fly kites."

He became a little dreamy, then went on.

"Auntie Kate murdered the champagne bottle, which was on our table at my request, with one glance. I ignored the look and popped the cork, smiling at her. I offered some to Bernard, Auntie Kate having made it abundantly clear that she would have none of it. 'Don't mind if I do,' Bernard said cheerfully. I was relieved to see him smile for a moment. 'Since we're here, we might as well have a little fun,' he said, tinkling his glass against mine as she watched in horror. Once we'd emptied our glasses, I asked her if she wanted something else and she ordered an ale. The band was on fire tonight, wasn't it? I could see Bernard's foot tapping the beat as he watched the crowd with a goofy smile. Clearly, Auntie Kate had nothing but disdain for everything and everyone she saw. Poor woman. I suppose her worst expectations about the theatre were coming true before her very eyes. It was a hot crowd, my goodness, lots of getting to know each other. I suppose the announcement at the beginning of the show came as a relief for her. Uncle Bernard sat up, ears pricked, as if someone was going to toss a ball for him to fetch. Sorry, it's wrong to talk like that, but he really was pathetic. Anyway, the show began, and it was quite a ride. At one point, I thought Auntie Kate was going to throw a tantrum. Such hatred, such anger!"

"But did she react to the show?"

"Yes, the show," he sighed and rolled his

eyes. "At first, she didn't say anything, but I could feel she was boiling. Bernard was like a boy in Hamleys. His eyes were sparkling and he was beaming, almost as if he knew his wife would be too busy being offended to notice he was having such a good time. Halfway through, she hissed into my ear, 'How can they? Skirts flying everywhere! Desecrating those uniforms, that's all they do! And that scenery! Those lights! Is this supposed to be a schoolyard? Where are the professors or the schoolmasters?'

"I was still trying to steer her towards amusement. 'Why? Do you want to see them spanked?'"

"You didn't!" I said, giggling.

"Yes, I did! Bernard, who heard me, laughed out loud. I thought I saw Katie turn purple in the dim light but as I sat between them, all she could do was turn away from the stage, a lonely face in an ocean of smiles and cheers, and sip her ale. Then the curtain came down. She tried to chastise Bernard over the loud interlude music. He pretended not to hear her and served us both another healthy helping of champagne. He tinkled his glass against mine again and turned expectantly towards the stage. The curtain rose on that lovely summertime park. Ron and his boys really outdid themselves."

"Yes, you can say that again. One of the girls is pregnant. Tina. He got to know her a little too well. And when he found out, he refused to help her."

"What a louse. I am so sorry. Tina's a lovely girl and she deserves to be treated much better," he said. "Bernard couldn't have enough of 'The Trouble with me is you', hooting and shouting and calling your name as soon as he recognised you."

"Did he see me winking at him?"

"Absolutely! He turned to me for a split second and sniggered. 'How vulgar,' Auntie Kate said before complaining, 'Now it's rings and see saws! What other excuses are they going to find to flash their underthings at this over excited crowd?'

"I couldn't help myself and said, 'If you think that's bad, wait until the next number auntie.' Gosh, it was a sight to behold, my aunt seeing all those naked girls dance to the sound of 'Penthouse Serenade'. Bernard was staring too. 'Lovely set,' he found the nerve to muster. I almost ruined the moment when Katie said to herself, in despair, 'But I love this song.'

"I wanted to laugh but it was clearly not the moment."

He paused, looking at me dreamily. "Bernard loved the beach. The waves and the girls tossing balls at each other in the next number. Katie didn't comment on the fact that the song was in German, but now that I think on it, she seemed much more disapproving of the English folk in the audience, happily singing along to 'Sommer, See und Sonnenschein' than the rowdy German sailors and distinguished German officers," he said, sighing in despair. "Bernard and I agreed that your colleagues made us want to go on a holiday. Is it just me or was the scene change a bit longer than the others?"

"Yeah, bloody sets, takes ages."

"It felt that way. Which means it felt double that long with Auntie Kate judging everyone around who was British and Uncle Bernard who was now quite drunk and making comments I didn't know he was capable of. Auntie Kate must've heard those comments before because all she did was roll her eyes and ask me how many more numbers we would have to sit through. I was glad to let her know that the next one was the last. She made her relief known, quite audibly. But I think I can honestly say that when the curtain finally rose, I heard her gasp under her breath. Uncle Bernard's admiration was a lot more audible. Now! The end of the evening! Auntie Kate wanted to be amongst the first ones out the door. I had told her you were going to join us and she gave me an earful about decency and times wasted and she departed. Uncle Bernard and I looked at each other, finished our glasses of champagne and wandered casually towards the exit. Auntie Kate was fuming at the street corner, tapping her foot and playing nervously with the strap of her purse. With barely a goodbye, she pushed Uncle Bernard in a cab and off they went."

"I see."

"Yes, that's why we weren't there where you came out."

"Thanks for the warning."

"I know, I am sorry to have left you in the middle of this mess, but I couldn't very well send them off like that, could I?"

"No, I suppose you're incapable of that."

"Thank you, you're too kind."

"And you had no choice."

"Right? How could it have gone any other way? I blame myself for that debacle."

"Don't be too harsh, she might have liked

it if she'd been a little more open minded."

"I suppose. Why am I not more like her? After all, she raised me."

"I get the distinct feeling, in that department, you inherited your uncle's enthusiasms."

"Uncle Bernard?" he laughed. "Yes, I suppose, after a while, maybe."

"How do you mean?"

"When I became a police officer, I was very green and full of Auntie Kate's principles. But then I began seeing all kinds of things, I met new people, I met you and those principles seemed far fetched in comparison with reality."

As we were staying at his place, near Aldersgate, we had all the time and all the room in the world to make love. Having said that, his flat was tiny, drafty and the walls patchy in colour, but he had no roommate. The neighbours were also quiet, mostly in the police force too. His bed was a tad wider than mine but our get togethers didn't require more than that. During that particular merging of our bodies, we were especially passionate and close and deep into each other. I didn't quite know why but there was something pressing in the air. Maybe it was all the sorry examples of sordid interaction or tepid marriages we saw. It made our love all the more precious. Maybe we both felt that pressure and worked at forgetting about it.

The next day, rain was pouring, despite it being July. As I was walking with him to the station, I had the feeling that our encounter had left a memory deep within me. I knew that it would grow to haunt me if I let nature run its course. Images of the Hackney Hospital flashed before my eyes. I suppressed any such memories before I became sick. Also, these visitations had been known to take care of themselves if the little visitor found the environment not to its liking. Whilst that might have been a sad experience for a couple looking to have a child, for a dancing girl, it was less so.

Early the next morning, I'd shown solidarity with his call to duty and had accompanied him all the way to the Yard. I even went as far as walking with him, huddled under a black umbrella, up to the broad, heavy doors. We came into the echoing entrance hall, leaving the watery sidewalk, him shaking the umbrella, me shaking my hair. The place, in spite of the premature hour, was bustling with its usual throng of busy constables, stern inspectors, guilty looking suspects and not quite sobered up arrests from the night before. In the midst of all this hustle and bustle, we held each other and looked into each other's eyes as if we were alone on a bridge in Paris. But just as we were about to kiss, perhaps because of that, someone caught up with us.

"Inspector, inspector!"

A constable approached.

"Yes?" Barney answered wearily, letting go of me and turning to his colleague.

"I am sorry for the intrusion, Inspector, but the chief said he wanted to see you the moment you came in."

"I'll be there momentarily," Barney said, about to turn back to me.

"No, inspector. He said immediately," the constable insisted.

"What could possibly be so urgent?" Barney said, losing patience.

Sometimes bobbies could be over diligent in passing on orders from the higher ranks of the Met. More than once had Barney dashed to someone's office when the reason hadn't been at all pressing.

"Inspector," he said in an excited if hushed

voice, looking at me over Barney's shoulder, "it's about the Higgins case. The girl, Barbara."

"What about her?" Barney asked, slightly more concerned.

"She's dead," the constable said.

"What?" I yelped.

"This is none of your business, Miss," the constable snapped, quite haughty.

"She's with me," Barney said by way of explanation, grabbing me by the arm and pulling me closer to him. "You can speak freely. What happened?"

"She was found dead this morning," the constable said slowly, for effect.

"And why does the chief want to see me?" Barney asked, lost in thought, letting go of my arm.

"To investigate, I suppose."

"Investigate? But surely the Hackney police will want to take care of that themselves."

"No, sir. The girl was released from hospital yesterday afternoon and went back to her old digs by the end of the day."

"And that's when she was found?" Barney asked, trying to compute all the new information into his working theory.

"Yes, sir, according to the lodger, she was found early this morning."

"What did she die of?"

"We don't know for sure yet, sir, but rumour has it that poison did her in."

"She was poisoned?"

"That's what the lodger said it looked like, but the coroner is on his way."

"Tell the chief I have gone to investigate and I'll phone in my report as soon as I know more."

Much to my delight, he grabbed my arm and dragged me behind him. As we hurried across the hall, he whispered, just loud enough I could hear him, "Poison is a woman's weapon, it doesn't make sense."

He was silent the rest of the way to Shoreditch which gave me plenty of time to review my theories. I had seen Barbara alive and well, or mostly well, at the Ivy House the day before yesterday. Who wanted her dead? Only one person's reputation and life's work hung in the balance if she was able to testify in court, that creep Higgins. But it was too obvious. He would have had plenty of time to use poison, in the knowledge she wouldn't stay forever in hospital. But wasn't it a bit radical? The step from fondling young girls to killing them because they wouldn't shut their trap was a considerable one. I'd met Higgins the day before and although he was a serious contender for the loony bin, I hadn't detected the passion it took to coldly plant poison in a girl's room. If he had, he would've had to be careful and quiet, making sure not to be seen. And where would he put the poison in the first place? This wasn't Louis XIVth's court, the art of poisoning garments was quite lost and out of fashion. Barney was right. Poison was a woman's murder weapon. With that comment, I could deduce that Barnaby's train of thought was going in the same direction as mine and he was equally impatient to arrive. I knew by seeing him fuming at the morning rush hour traffic slowing us down. No amount of scowling at his wristwatch would help matters either. I was happy.

He noticed me looking at him and smiled, taking my hand and kissing it.

"I am glad you're here," he said.

"I am surprised to be, you always say I distract you from work. I am glad you changed your mind about that."

"I haven't, actually," he said. "It's just that you were there and I'd made all this fuss about you being with me. I couldn't very well leave you at the station, could I?"

"It certainly sounds like I was an essential part of this little expedition," I said, pouting and looking out at the window.

"I am joking," he said, sliding to my side of the cab's backseat and putting his arm around my waist. "I am glad you're here now. Your feminine intuition is going to help me solve this."

"Don't get your hopes up," I sighed. "I'm as perplexed as you are at the presence of poison."

"As long as you're not too perplexed at the presence of a poisoned corpse, we'll be fine," he said with a wink as we were approaching the busy sidewalk.

He jumped on the curb and held the door open for me. The usual crowd of gawkers, mostly made of 'fallen' girls and orphans, were held back by a couple of bobbies on either side of the door. In rags and malnourished, they yelled complaints and random questions at anyone who would listen. The building's entrance, thus protected, looked worse than I imagined. It had taken tremendous hope into the architects of yore to put up this shack and believe it would see its tenth anniversary. By my count, it could collapse anytime.

While Barney got the report from the constables, I walked slowly towards the door, trying to memorise all the faces in the small crowd in front of the sordid house. Although Barnaby and I had a strong inkling who the culprit might be, I thought I'd keep a wary eye out anyway. It was common knowledge that perpetrators stayed in the vicinity of the crime if they were bold enough to believe they would not be found out. The newspaper headlines about Barbara and Father Higgins had been broad and brash enough to invite a company of jealous orphans, envious comrades or greedy thieves. Hence, Higgins' guilt was not absolutely certain. Yet.

Our unspoken working theory was that Higgins was guilty, but I wanted to be prepared in case a more original breed of wrongdoer presented themselves. It goes without saying that none of the nosy neighbours had looked like a poisoner to me. If only it were that easy to solve crimes.

Barney joined me and we entered the front door under a shower of rain and almost as many yelled questions and rude innuendoes. I wish I could say I was relieved to be inside but that would be a lie.

How could anyone breathe in this place? Let alone live? It was a typically Victorian house with stairs shooting up almost from the front door, two rooms off to the left and the kitchen at the back looking out into the garden. Everything was soiled. The leaks in the roof had bled all the way down the wallpaper of the entrance hall leaving large V shaped designs from the ceiling to the floor. The carpet was almost black for all the dust and dirt it retained. The windows were grimy. Paint was peeling off the door frames and the stairs balustrade. It must have been rather nice when it was first built, but it was run down beyond repair.

Barnaby and I exchanged dismayed glances just as the lodger, Mrs Daws, walked in, wiping her calloused hands on her dirty apron. She had a few teeth missing and her grey hair was pinned up in a drunken bird's nest.

"What is it?" she asked in a rough voice.

"I am sorry to disturb you," Barney said, tremendously polite and soft spoken, "I am inspector Cumberland. I'm here to investigate the death of Miss Scott. Are you the owner of this establishment?" he asked, checking his notes, although he knew her to be running a dirty operation, in more ways than one. "Mrs Daws?"

She eyed his notes before looking us both over with suspicion, as if we were trespassing. "Who's she?" she asked as if she had detected competition for her girls in some way. I almost responded but Barnaby put his strong hand on my arm and squeezed it.

"She is my assistant, Miss Turner," he said apologetically. "Could we see the room?"

"It's upstairs," she said, and led the way, dragging her broad behind and club foot slowly to the first floor.

On the landing, three doors were slightly ajar with a frightened face peeking through the cracks. The state of cleanliness here was worse than downstairs, a smell of decay and human waste having been added for good measure.

"The girls are frightened," she rasped.

"Did any of them know Father Higgins?" Barney asked, following the disagreeable woman closely along the landing's balustrade, trying not to touch anything.

"Most of them. Why do you want to know?" she asked, stopping dead in her tracks and turning to face him.

"I..." Barnaby stuttered as he was taken

aback by the sudden surge of intuition. "I know that he'd visited Barbara, here, some time ago, and I was wondering whether he'd visited anyone else, during that time, or before, or after? Do you know him well?" he asked, out of breath, perspiring under his hat.

"Not so much. Some of the girls did. We all thought he was the nice sort, you see. Before, you know?"

She saw she had put her lurid point across and started a slow journey up the next flight of stairs with a despondent grunt. Barney rolled his eyes, putting his fingers to his nose, as if to block a bad smell, but he couldn't because he had his notepad in one hand and his pencil in the other. I smiled encouragingly at him and winked.

She reached the bathroom landing with a wheezing sound that was starting to alarm me. The dampness on the walls was not of any comfort either. The bathroom door was open and the sights and smells coming from there I did not associate with bathing or cleaning oneself.

"Where do the girls get the money to pay the rent?" Barnaby asked, perfectly calm in spite of the climb and the eagerness to get to Barbara's room.

"Most of them have a benefactor in the upper crust, you see," she said, pausing for a moment for a breather. "But it's all honourable gents and ladies, people who want to help the less fortunate. Charity like, you see?"

"I see," Barney said. "Not a bad deal for you either, right?"

"I don't know what you're talking about," she sniffed.

"Can we see the room now?" he said.

She gathered what seemed like the rest of her life's energy and started shuffling along, slowly climbing to the next landing.

It, too, had three white doors and plenty of stains on the once whitewashed walls. Here, only two of them were concealing a frightened observer as the third one was wide open. Everywhere, there were traces of vermin, bugs, beetles and rot. Following her demonstrative gesture, Barnaby and I cautiously entered the room. The wench grunted one last time and commenced her descent.

"There's not enough room to swing a cat in here," I commented as I noted the unmade bed, the grey-green walls, the minute window, the cracks in the ceiling and the dirty carpet.

Barney was at the other end of the room, silently observing the corpse covered in a very white sheet.

"Yes, it's like dying in a coffin," he murmured as if to himself.

As I reached his side, he crouched and threw back the part of the sheet covering her face. I must admit, I jumped back. I consider myself a well-travelled, hardened adventurer but I had never seen the face of a poisoned person before. It was gruesome. Her eyes were open with a look of frozen terror. Her eyelids and sockets were dark blue. But what startled me most were the chequered teeth beneath drawn back lips and gums. She looked to be in perpetual agony. And there was frothing at the lips, like a mad animal. It was truly disturbing. I had to look away and say something.

"What kind of poison does that?"

"Pretty standard arsenic," said the coroner, standing on the door step.

Barnaby covered the ashen face and got up.

"But the frothing? Is that standard?"

"No, inspector, that's not frothing, that's tooth powder. Look, she's still holding the toothbrush," he said, crossing the room and lifting the sheet above her stiff right hand. Sure enough, Barbara was clutching her wooden toothbrush.

"Anything else you can tell me?" Barney asked as the coroner was making his way to the door, somewhat hastily.

"The poison was mixed in the tooth powder or placed on the toothbrush. It must have acted quickly since it got into the blood through the gums. She didn't feel much of anything."

I thought that to be an optimistic opinion given the mask of horror and pain etched on her face, under that sheet.

"Thank you, doctor," Barnaby said.

"You're welcome," the doctor said, a little surprised and made to leave before turning around, popping his head only through the doorframe. "Her flatmate, next door, has quite the story. I went to that room looking for a wash basin. By the way, would you be so kind as to put that toothbrush in an evidence bag and bring it to the Yard whenever you make it back?" he added with a meaningful glance in my direction.

And he was gone. Barnaby winked at me and the vexation I'd felt by the doctor's suggestive remark vanished.

I watched Barney carefully opening the grip of her fingers as *rigor mortis* was starting to set in, and meticulously putting the toothbrush in one of the paper bags he always had in his pockets. Sometimes he even used them to store the sweets he bought for me on his way to my apartment, which was odd and practical, but quite all right. Even though he was crouching, and I stood over him, I could see the remains of white powder on the single brushes. They would disperse in the bag, but no finger prints could be lifted off the wooden handle, so it didn't matter all that much. Barney stood up and looked down at me with a smile.

"This is all very exciting to you, isn't it?"

"Yes. Not to you?" I asked, raising my eyebrows.

"Not quite as much, I don't think. For one thing, it's my job so I shouldn't let it affect me and I don't see the excitement. This poor girl is dead! Don't you care?"

"I do. Barney don't make me out to be heartless. I was surprised when we heard the news and quite frightened when I saw her face. But now, unless I am much mistaken, we have enough evidence to put Higgins behind bars."

"What on Earth makes you think that? Dozens of suspects spring to mind. Another one of the girls - in these parts, they kill you for the pettiest reasons - another of her gents, perhaps. It is very possible that Higgins wasn't her only 'benefactor' and, with his arrest in the papers, she became available and famous. Or it might've been suicide…"

"Suicide? That's absurd."

"Why? You told me the hospital where she spent the last few days was sordid. Maybe she had an epiphany and realized the error of her ways and decided to make amends?"

"By killing herself? Do me a favour. If she was repentant, she would've joined a convent. And suicide by poisoning? That would mean a guilty conscience indeed. And where would a girl like that get arsenic?"

"Rat poison," he said, a little unnerved by my resisting his theory. "You spoke to her. Did she seem repentant, suicidal or otherwise?"

"She seemed like her old self. I didn't know her, but she had spunk and wanted to live and get her share of a good time. No, suicide is not an option."

"Fine," Barney sighed. "Let's go talk to that flatmate of hers, maybe she can clear things up for us."

Barnaby led the way and I followed, having given up the act of looking like I was tough enough to stand the smell and taken out a handkerchief to put in front of my nose and mouth. In spite of it being mid morning, the corridor was gloomy and muggy. All imaginable human smells were starting to intensify on the landing. Each room had a little window, but no draft reached the core of the house, except in the winter I guessed.

Barnaby knocked on the door and the girl opened immediately as if she had been waiting for us. The walls were probably wafer thin and she had heard our debate. I felt bad for a moment, this girl's life was in all probability as despondent as poor Barbara's.

"Hello," Barney said, taking off his hat. "I am Inspector Cumberland, and this is my assistant, Mrs Turner."

"That's funny," she said, looking at us like a custom's officer eyeing a suspicious package.

Her shoulder length hair was black and in bad need of a wash. She wore a linen night gown that required the attention of a laundress - or the handler of the basement furnace. Her knit jacket was a convenient grey, so its dustiness was harder to spot. Her scuffed black leather shoes were two sizes too big for her. If it hadn't been for her glare and the circumstances, they would almost have been comical.

I had been mistaken. This girl was much worse off than Barbara. I wasn't surprised Higgins hadn't shown an interest in her. For one thing, the hair was the wrong colour. Then her eyes had no fire, no will to live. She moved slowly, as if life's currents were shaping her every movement. But her voice was like clogs over gravel, loud, brash and hostile.

"How do you mean?" Barney said, putting a lot of warmth in his tone, no doubt to tame the beast. I am not of a jealous nature, most of the time. I knew for certain that she wasn't his type. But I was about her age when we first met and almost in as pitiful a situation. I didn't like his tone one bit.

"That's your bird or I am the Queen of Shiva."

"All right then, she's more than my assistant," Barnaby conceded smiling. "But she's a good detective and she's here to help me find who killed Barbara. Do you…"

"Oh! So that's what happened?" she said.

Much to my surprise, I saw her fight back tears and I heard her voice choke up. With slow gestures, she sat on the tiny bed and covered her face with her hands, crying silently.

"Is it all right if we come in?" Barney asked softly.

I admired the way he stuck to the procedures, given the situation. My first instinct would have been to sit on that bed and put my arm around her. I probably wouldn't have done it though because she was so dirty and unpredictable. I remained motionless.

Her tears had left two light streaks on her cheeks. She stared at us with big brown eyes as if she didn't know what to do in her despair. She nodded and we silently entered the room and closed the door.

The pale daylight struggled to reach inside the glum room. The bed was taking up most of the space and a small sink adorned one corner while a minute window had been pierced in the opposite wall, an afterthought.

Barnaby stood opposite her while I remained close to the door. The carpet had the colour and feel of a mossy forest floor. The sheets were beige, distant cousin of the white they used to be. The rain, still pouring outside, was making its way into the building by running along the wall in silent rivulets.

"I should've known. I should've said som'ing," she uttered as she looked at each of us in turn, not knowing who ought to hear her confession. All trace of her earlier bravado was entirely gone.

"What do you know? What should you have said?" Barney asked cautiously, her eyes settling on him, forgetting me for the most part of what followed.

"I knew he was a bad sort. I'd met him a few times on the landing. Mind you, I don't blame her. A girl's got to have something to survive. I don't look nice enough, not like Barbara," she whimpered. "She wasn't like the rest of us, she had dreams, she knew she wasn't stayin' 'ere long and she was 'appy for others to carry the can if it went her way. I 'ad to explain the presence of a man in her room to the bloody landlady a few times."

"I'm sorry," interrupted Barney, coming straight to the point. "Do you have any information regarding the death of Barbara Harris?"

"Do I? Of course, I do. That's why you're here."

She blabbered on. It was like watching

someone's train of thought without any filter. If she was ever to testify, they would have to start in the morning or they wouldn't be done by teatime. With gentle coaxing and encouraging redirection, Barnaby finally got her on the right track.

"I was really sad to see Barbara go when she did. She was a bit of a selfish slag but if any loot came her way, she always made sure I had a bit of it too. So, when the police came to put her in the hospital, I was worried. For her protection they said, my eye! It was some sort of women's prison, for sure."

I shuddered at the thought of Barbara in that bed, in that hospital, begging me to help her.

"It all got much more quiet like, after she'd gone. None of the others know how to pick 'em up the way she did. And we had no news either. The blasted landlady said they talked about her in the papers, but we shouldn't concern ourselves with 'such things', she said, the old hag. Of course it concerns us! Of course it's our business!"

"Had you met the last gentleman who visited Barbara?"

"Gentleman! My eye! He was dressed like a priest all right, but I saw the shine in his eye.

He wasn't here to convert no one."

"So, you did meet him?"

"Of course! That's how I recognised him yesterday morning, when he came to her room."

After ten minutes of rambling nonsense, the breather which followed that statement should have been welcome, but it only left room for the echo of its implications which rang like a cannonade. I clutched my handkerchief so tightly, it hurt. I felt my heart beating madly, colour rising to my cheeks. There it was. That scum Higgins had done it!

After he had caught his breath, Barnaby gave me a brief smile of victory. If we could get her to say what she knew coherently in court, we had a witness who placed Higgins in the girl's room only a couple of hours before she poisoned herself with the arsenic laced toothbrush.

"So, to be clear, you saw him yesterday?" Barney asked slowly.

"Yes," she said before the whimpering and wiggling started again. "I saw him leave. I'd heard someone go into the room, real early like. I almost shouted for Barbara to pipe down because I'd 'ad a late night, you know, working. At first, I thought it was the landlady getting the rest of Barbara's things, but then I heard noises, here and there, and the water tap turning. I got up and looked through the keyhole. For sure, there he was, real careful to close the door without a sound. I watched him walk down the corridor and go down the stairs. I thought nothing of it, he might've left some of his private things in the room and he'd be wanting them back. I never imagined he would do this. Barbara, poor Barbara."

The rest of her confused wails were lost in the folds of the jacket she used to wipe her face and blow her nose.

"Thank you, Miss... Miss?"

"Bradstreet, Clementine Bradstreet. But everyone calls me Clem."

"Thank you, Miss Bradstreet. We will have a man at the door so you will be quite safe here, until you are called to testify."

Before she could protest, Barnaby had stepped out of the stuffy room, pushing me delicately in front of him.

"We have to get out here, the stench is choking me," he whispered as he kept moving towards the stairs. I laughed until we were out on the street, as much because of his joke than because of the loosening tension and the overwhelming feeling of triumph. We huddled under an umbrella, smiling and breathing the fresh air.

"So? What do you think?" I said.

"What do I think?" he said, raising his eyebrows. "I think we've got him where we want him."

"But why? I mean, why did he do it?"

"Yes, that's where various options present themselves."

"Various? I thought it was obvious. He must've heard she was going home and he was frightened she would testify against him."

"But at worst, he would be defrocked and have to go back to his former life. Do you know what that was, by the way?"

"No idea," I sighed, quite befuddled by the question. "Selling children's toys?"

"Almost," Barnaby laughed. "He was a circus performer."

"You're joking?"

"Not at all. Quite successful, too."

"Whatever possessed him to go into priesthood?"

"No one knows. He might've started helping girls in the circus and he wanted to do more."

"Nicely put," I said in disdain, thinking of

Barbara and all the other girls that he must have 'saved'.

We were still walking under the umbrella and the downpour.

"Why are we not in a dry, warm cab?"

"I know a pub down the road that serves a decent lunch. I want to ask around about Higgins and Barbara."

"All right," I said, pulling him tighter against my side. "As we are out for a walk, tell me, what other options could there possibly be to explain why a man shows up at a girl's boarding house at the crack of dawn with arsenic in his pocket?"

"Rat poison," Barney corrected me.

"But the doctor said arsenic."

"It was the arsenic in the rat poison that killed her. Arsenic alone is quite difficult to get, and pharmacists ask a lot of questions, whereas any household has rat poison."

"All right, our man shows up with rat poison in his pocket. He goes up two flights of stairs undetected and then what? Did he know he was going to put it on the toothbrush?"

"I don't know," Barnaby said gently. "I suppose we'll have to ask him when we arrest him this afternoon."

"He hesitated," I said, "the water pitcher or the toothbrush."

"Or the bed cushion. There have been cases where the poison was reduced to a thin powder and spread on the sheets and the cushion."

"How far it is to that bloody pub? My feet will be soaking wet."

"Not long now. Come on, Mrs Watson, what possible other motive could he have had. Remember that, as you have aptly pointed out, this was very much a premeditated crime."

"I'll say! But why? He was taking an awful risk. I mean the early hours of the morning is when the girls are knocked out from whatever they did the night before. But still..."

"Absolutely."

"So? Go on. I am drenched, bored and cold. Don't keep me guessing."

"All right. We've established that he found religion late in life and that his target for redemption was dubious at best. So a not entirely stable mind is to be expected. We might even go further and say that he was carried here by a wave of fervour. Maybe he thought that if he couldn't save Barbara, no one could. He probably assumed that her returning to the boarding house meant she would go back to her evil ways. And he didn't want to see another soul lost to the downfall awaiting her in that place. Or he was disappointed she had told on him after all he had done for her. Or he was simply jealous."

He took a deep breath after this long explanation. He looked at me proudly. All I could do was raise an eyebrow, doubting my boyfriend's sanity for a moment.

"I hope the place we're going to has rooms to rent because, after this dreadful walk and absurd diatribe, I will have to get out of these wet clothes, and you will have to keep me entertained."

Barnaby roared with laughter as he opened the pub's old wooden doors to let me pass. I am glad to say that, after a healthy meal, he did.

BASED ON A TRUE STORY

THE MURDER

In February 1932, a story was published about a priest citing his supposed behaviour with women in London. Thus the church was unable to suppress the case to be scrutinized by a consistory court in March. After long deliberation, in July, the court found him guilty on five counts of immorality and was defrocked. His only recourse was to return to Blackpool and resume his career as a showman.

THE THEATRE

The Windmill Theatre — now The Windmill International — in Great Windmill Street, London was for many years both a variety and revue theatre. The Windmill remains best known for its nude *tableaux vivants*, which began in 1932 (…) In 1930, Laura Henderson bought the Palais de Luxe building and hired Howard Jones, an architect, to remodel the interior to a small 320-seat, one-tier theatre. It was then renamed the Windmill. It opened on 22 June 1931, as a playhouse (…)

www.en.wikipedia.org/wiki/Windmill_TheatrE

Secrets of a Dancing Girl

The Series

1. The Chess Player
2. A Mouthful of Bread
3. One of Us
4. My Lover
5. The Priest
6. Hunger March

http://www.secretsofadancinggirl.co.uk/